First published in the United States, Great Britain, Canada, Australia, and New Zealand in 2009
by North-South Books Inc., an imprint of NordSüd Verlag AG, CH-8005 Zürich, Switzerland.
Distributed in the United States by North-South Books Inc., New York 10001.

Library of Congress Cataloging-in-Publication Data is available.
ISBN: 978-0-7358-2259-7 (trade edition).
10 9 8 7 6 5 4 3 2 1
Printed in Belgium

www.northsouth.com

FSC
Mixed Sources
Product group from well-managed
forests and other controlled sources

Cert no. BV-COC-070303
www.fsc.org
© 1996 Forest Stewardship Council

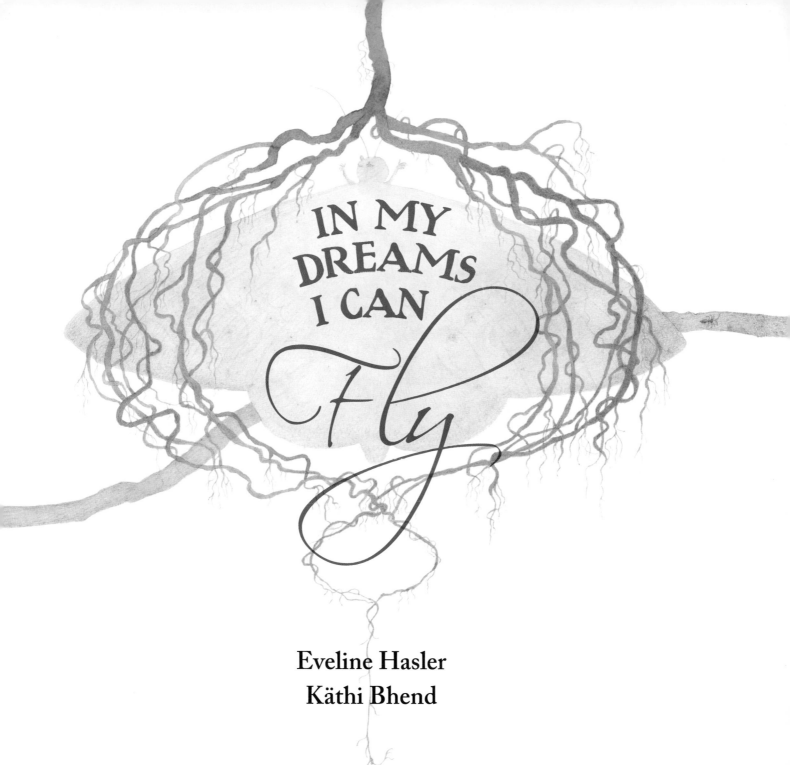

IN MY DREAMS I CAN Fly

Eveline Hasler

Käthi Bhend

NorthSouth
New York / London

Above the ground,
a strong wind was blowing
the leaves from the trees.
Fall had arrived.

Below the ground,
five friends were getting ready
for the long cold winter ahead:

a grub,

two worms,
a beetle,

and a caterpillar.

Their homes were connected by tunnels.

Every third evening, the friends played cards together in the grub's home among the roots. The little beetle usually lost, so the caterpillar told him funny stories and jokes to cheer him up.

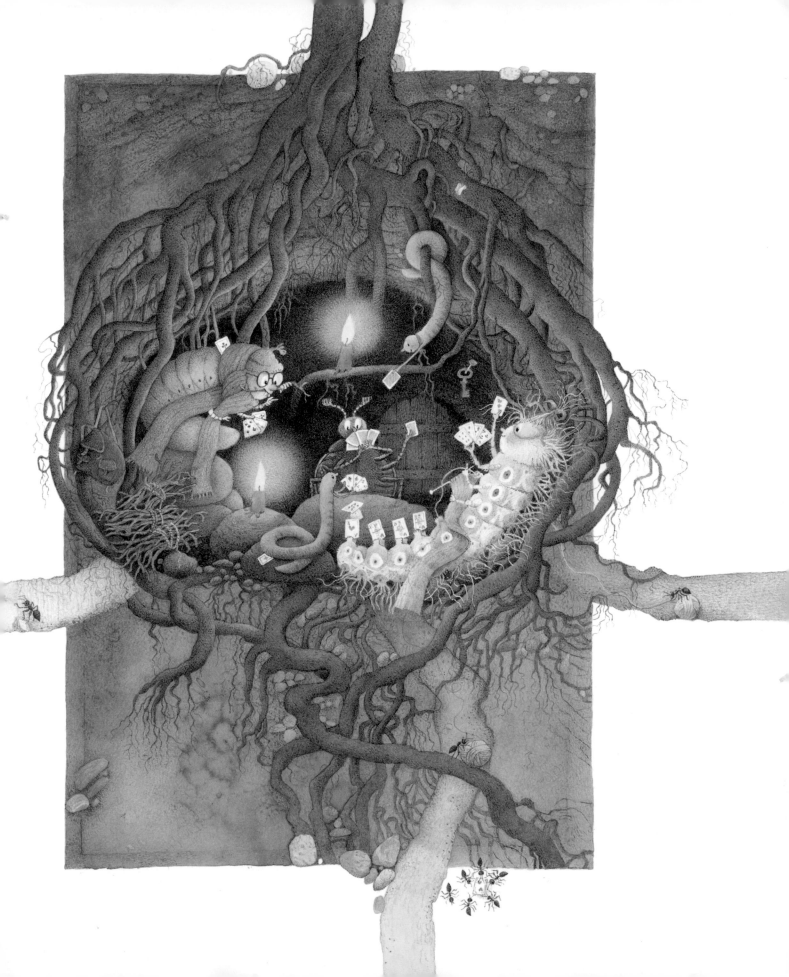

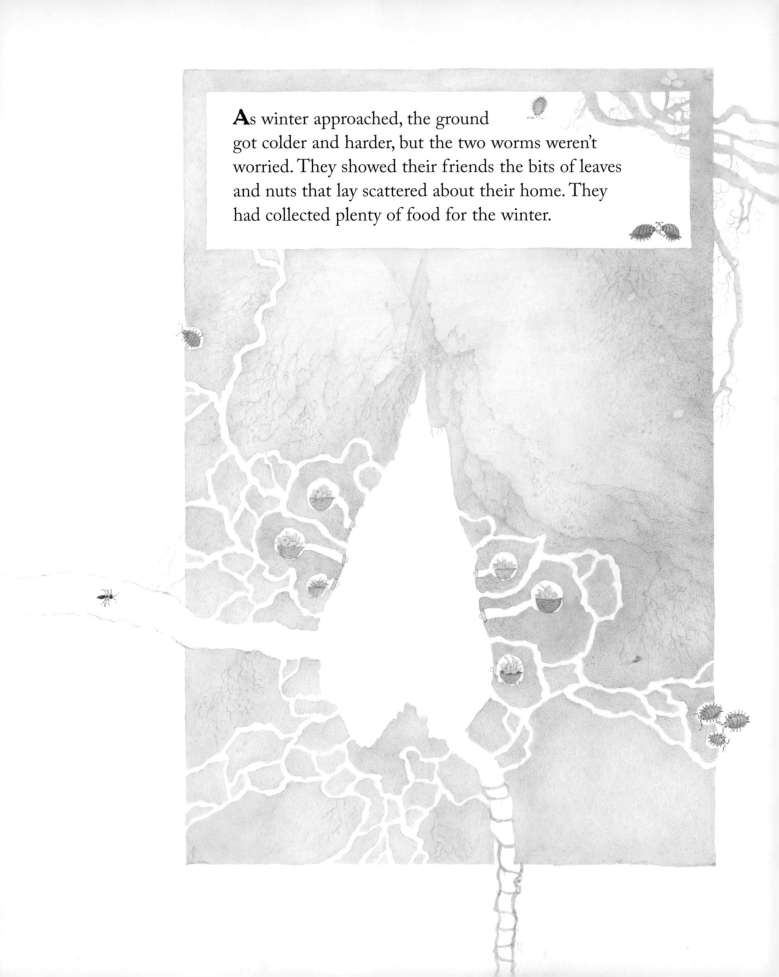

As winter approached, the ground
got colder and harder, but the two worms weren't
worried. They showed their friends the bits of leaves
and nuts that lay scattered about their home. They
had collected plenty of food for the winter.

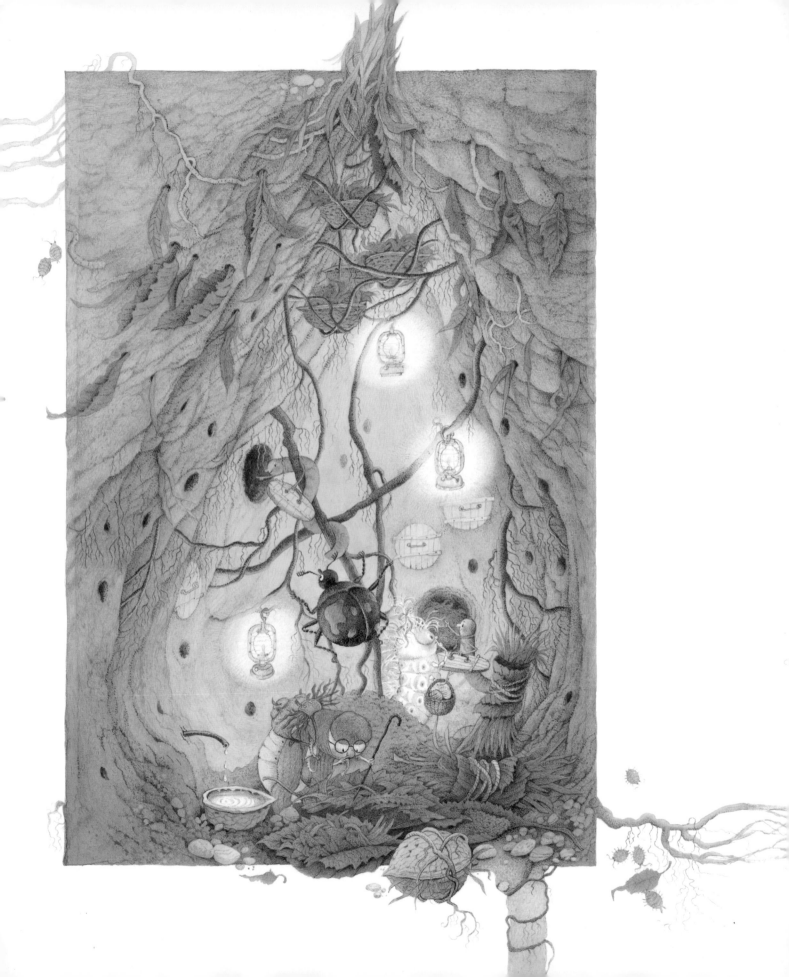

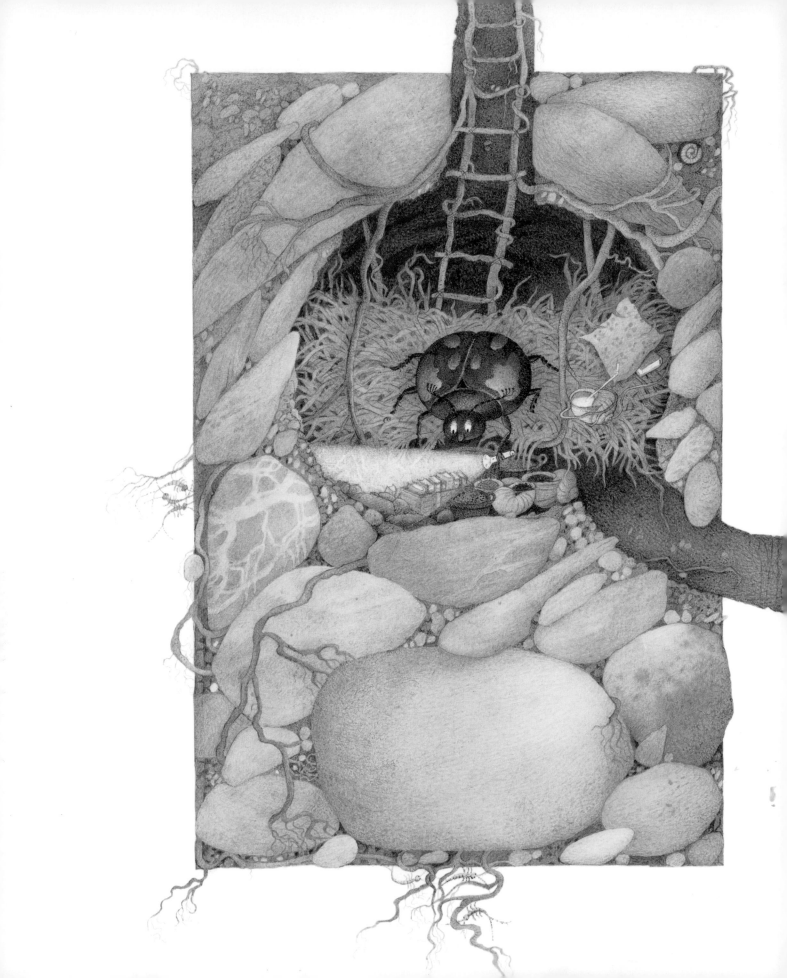

"I'm not worried about winter either!" cried the beetle, whose home was as round as he was. "Look at the tasty morsels I've hidden under my bed. No one will steal them from me!"

"What about you?" the friends asked the caterpillar. "What have you saved?"

"Come with me and I'll show you," said the caterpillar, and she led the way through a tunnel.

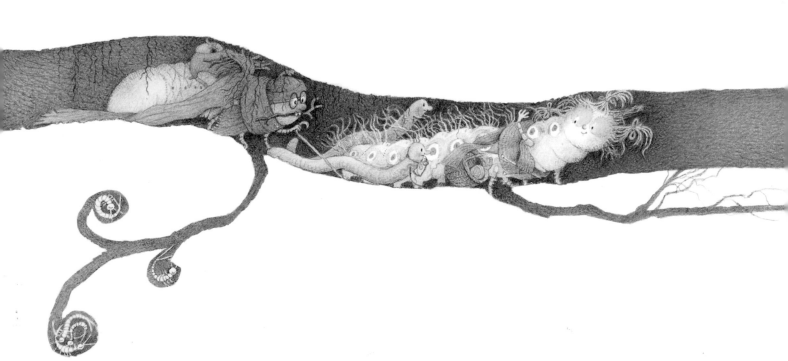

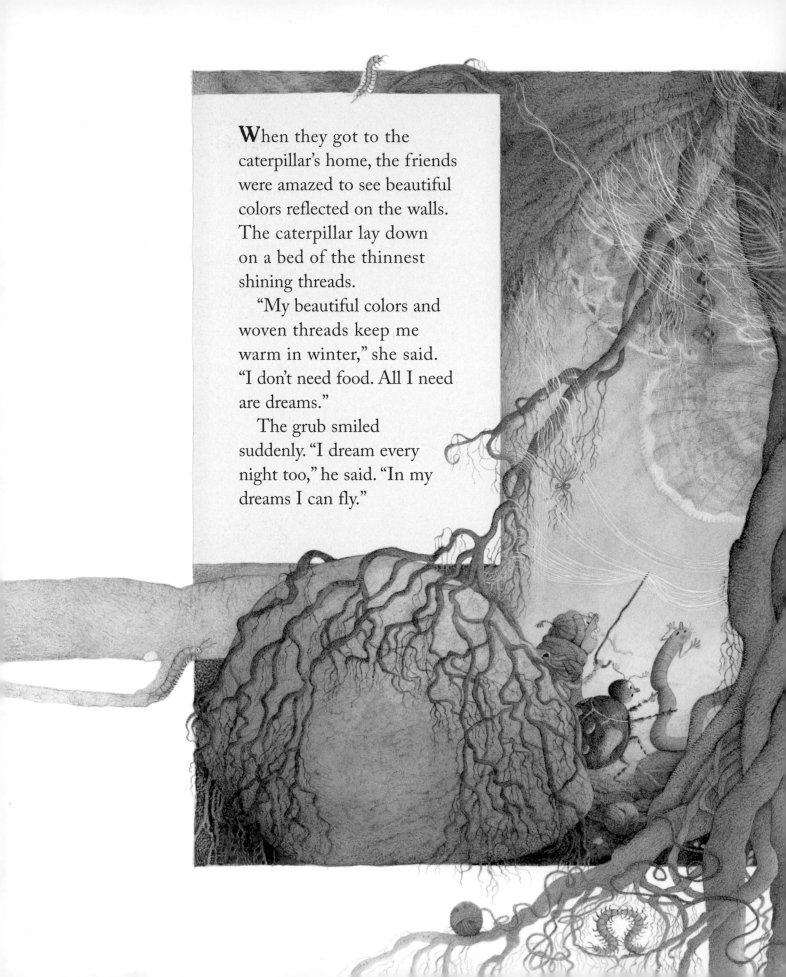

When they got to the caterpillar's home, the friends were amazed to see beautiful colors reflected on the walls. The caterpillar lay down on a bed of the thinnest shining threads.

"My beautiful colors and woven threads keep me warm in winter," she said. "I don't need food. All I need are dreams."

The grub smiled suddenly. "I dream every night too," he said. "In my dreams I can fly."

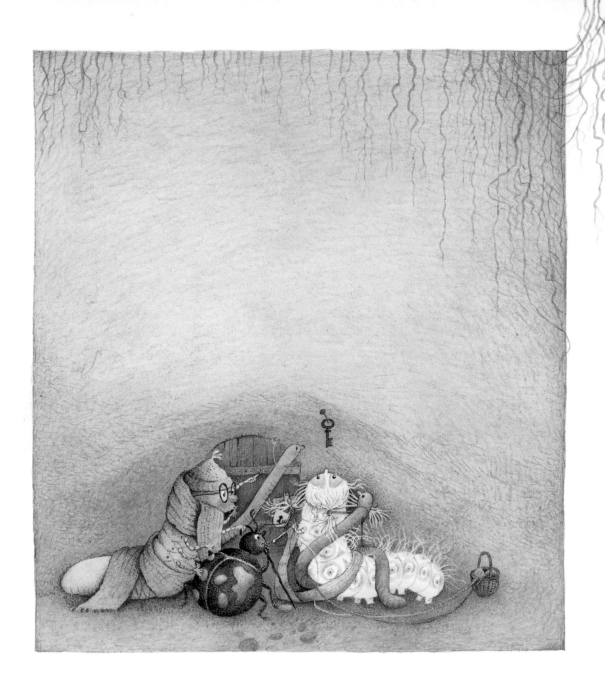

"I have something saved for winter too," the grub continued.
"But it's a secret. I'm saving it for when we've eaten everything else.
Then we can eat my secret together."

The grub showed them the door to his storeroom. It was locked,
but the key was hanging above the door.

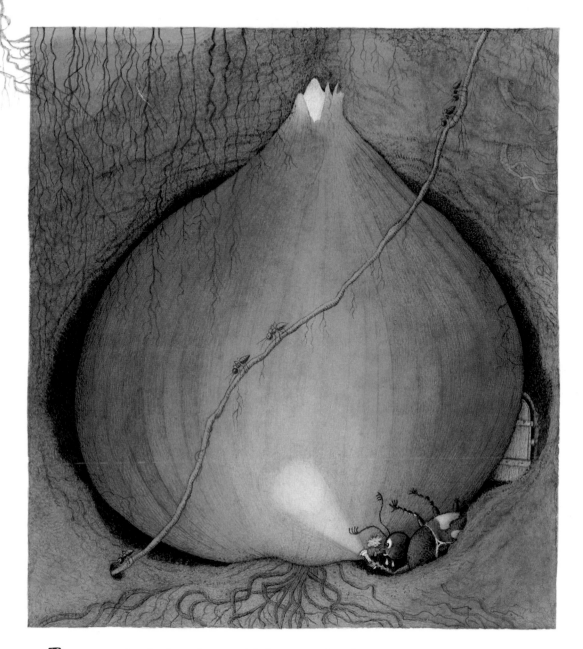

The poor little beetle couldn't stop thinking about what might be hidden behind that door. One afternoon, when the grub had gone out, he took the key and unlocked the door. Inside was a huge onion!

The beetle's mouth started to water. That onion looked so big and juicy! Right at the bottom, where no one would notice, he nibbled a little bit away.

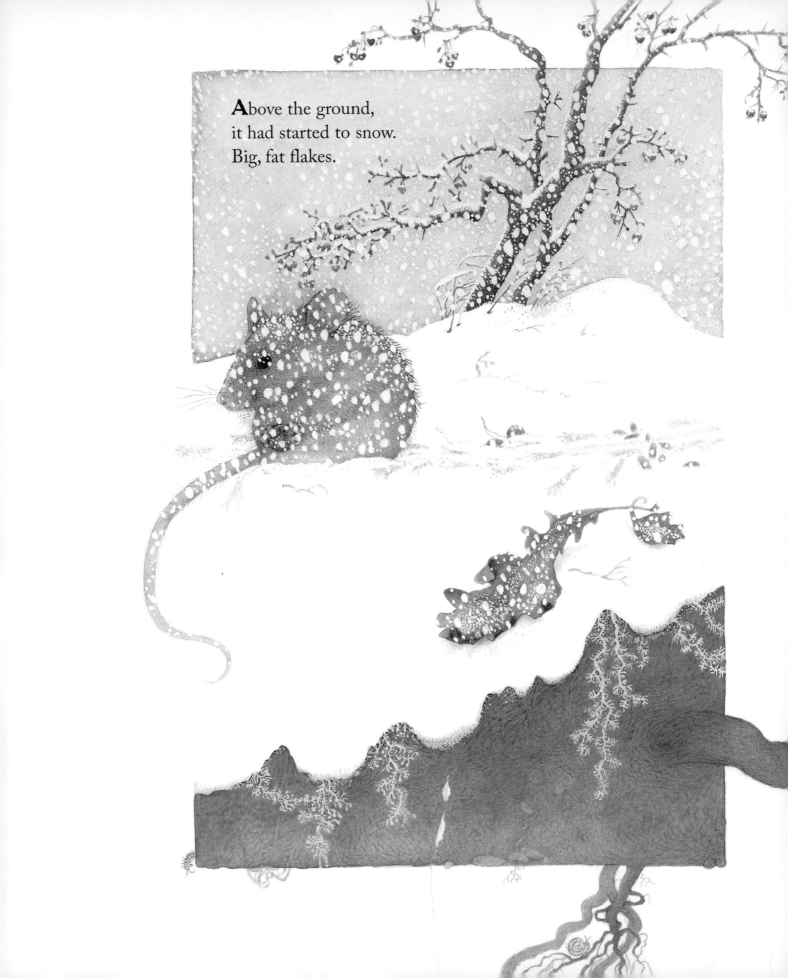

Above the ground,
it had started to snow.
Big, fat flakes.

That evening, the friends gathered to play cards, but the caterpillar wasn't among them.

The beetle went to look for her. He found the caterpillar in her room, wrapped in thousands of tiny threads.

"Why are you hiding?" asked the beetle. "Come on. We're playing cards!"

"I'm dreaming," the caterpillar whispered, so softly that the little beetle could scarcely hear her.

"What are you dreaming about?" asked the beetle.

"About colors and sky," came the soft reply.

The beetle hurried back to tell his friends about the caterpillar. "Perhaps she just needs a rest," said the grub. "Don't worry. She'll feel better soon."

It seemed as if spring would never come. It was getting very cold under the ground. And the friends were running out of food.

"I think it's time to show you my secret," said the grub one evening. He took the key down from the wall and opened the door to his storeroom.

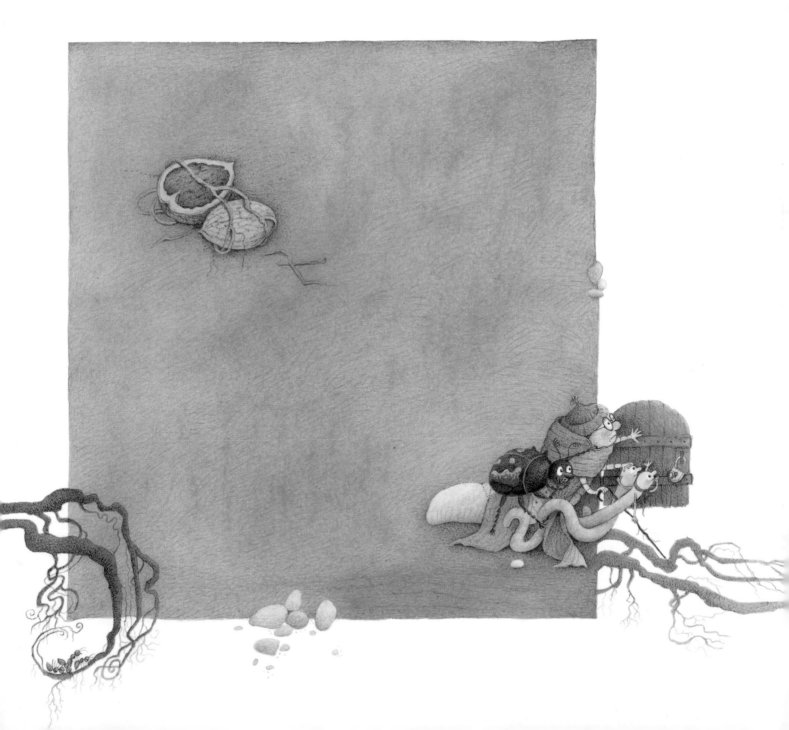

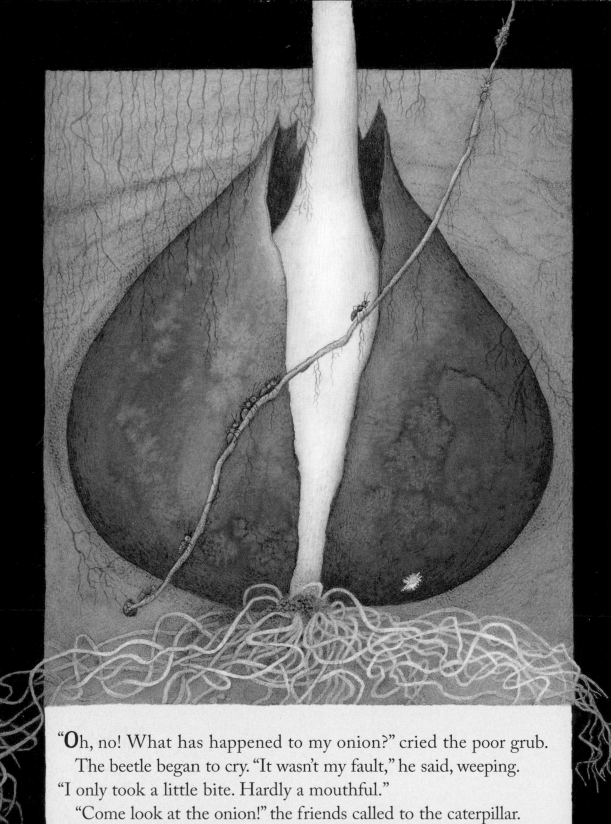

"Oh, no! What has happened to my onion?" cried the poor grub.
    The beetle began to cry. "It wasn't my fault," he said, weeping.
"I only took a little bite. Hardly a mouthful."
    "Come look at the onion!" the friends called to the caterpillar.

But the caterpillar did not come. In her home they discovered only a tightly woven ball.

It was empty.

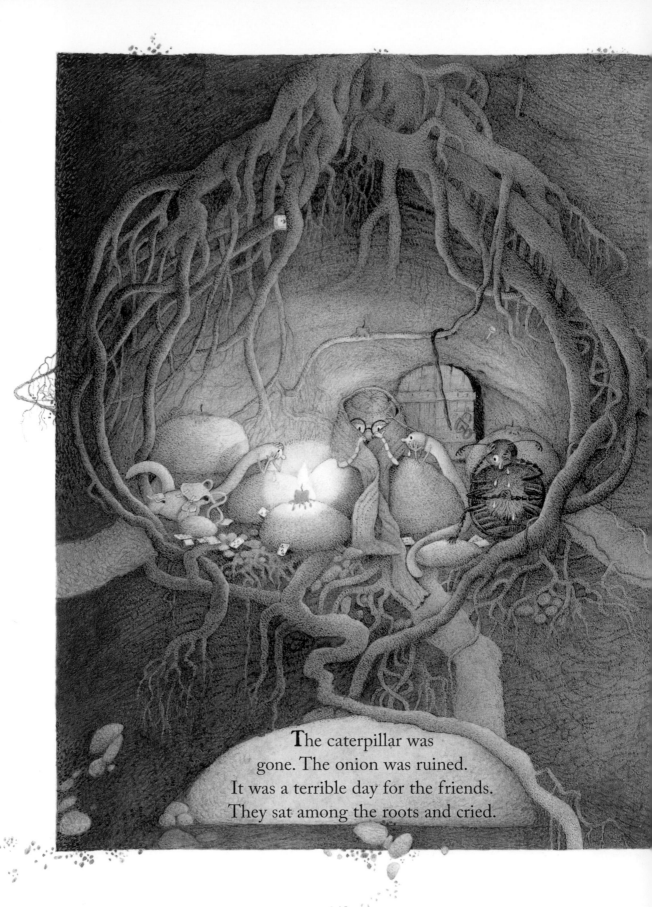

The caterpillar was
gone. The onion was ruined.
It was a terrible day for the friends.
They sat among the roots and cried.

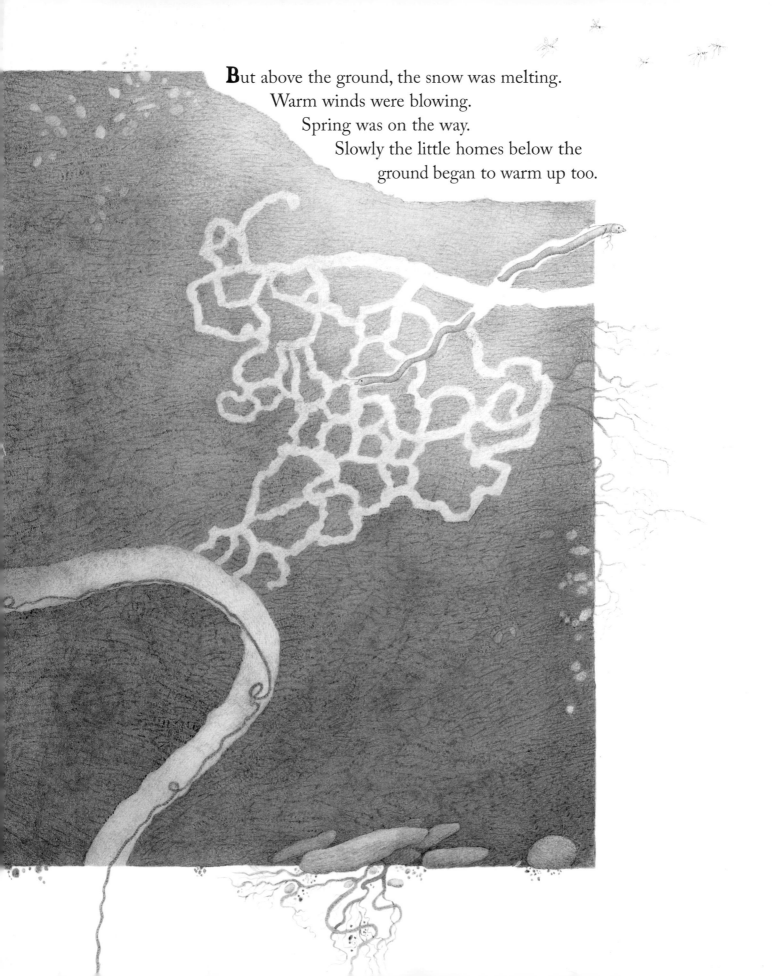

But above the ground, the snow was melting.
Warm winds were blowing.
Spring was on the way.
Slowly the little homes below the
ground began to warm up too.

The two worms felt perky again. They began to dig tunnels all over the place.

Suddenly one popped his head through the ground into the fresh air and sunshine.

"There's a whole new world up here!" he said.

Right above the grub's storeroom stood a tall green stem with a bright bud on top.

"You've got to come up and see this!" he called.

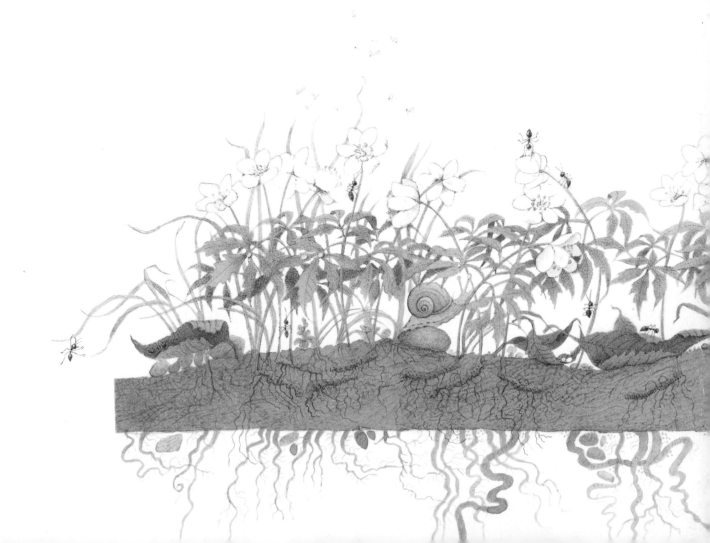

The worms raced back with their news.

"Your onion isn't dead after all," they told the grub. "Something amazing has happened to it!"

The grub set off to see for himself. Slowly he worked his way up . . . and up . . .

By the time he got to the surface, it was night. There was the beautiful flower, stretching up above him.

"Hello, Grub!" said a voice in the air.

The grub would have recognized that voice anywhere. It was the caterpillar! But she wasn't a caterpillar any more.

"You can fly!" gasped the grub. "It's what I've always dreamed of doing."

The butterfly laughed. "Be patient, little grub," she said softly. "One day your dream will come true!"